This book belongs to

DISNEY'S
THE EMPEROR'S
NEW GROOVE

A READ-ALOUD STORYBOOK

Adapted by Natalye Abuan

Illustrated by the artists at Disney Publishing Creative Development:
Ken Becker, Judie Clarke, Samantha Clarke, Domino Dai,
Caroline Egan, Brent Ford, Todd Ford, Atelier Philippe Harchy,
Denise Shimabukuro, Elizabeth Tate, Scott Tilley, Lori Tyminski.

MOUSE WORKS

Find us at www.disneybooks.com for more Mouse Works fun!

Printed in the United States of America.

ISBN 0-7364-0196-2

Spoiled Rotten

Once upon a time, there was a magnificent empire run by Emperor Kuzco. Let's face it: Kuzco was spoiled, rude, and totally obnoxious. And those were his good qualities!

Kuzco had an adviser named Yzma.
She was nasty to all the peasants.
Yzma's assistant was a strong young
man named Kronk. He did things
like swat flies for Yzma—even
if it meant swatting his own
forehead. Duh!

Yzma's idea of fun was to sit on Kuzco's throne and pretend to run the empire. This really annoyed Kuzco. So one day he fired her! Yzma was *not* happy about that.

Later that day, a peasant named Pacha was called in to see Kuzco.

Kuzco told Pacha he was going to destroy his village to build a vacation home called Kuzcotopia.

"But where will the people of my village live?" the gentle peasant asked in dismay.

"Hmm," Kuzco said selfishly. "Don't know. Don't care."

What's for Dinner?

Meanwhile, Yzma and Kronk plotted a way to get rid of Kuzco.

"I'll just poison him!" Yzma cried.

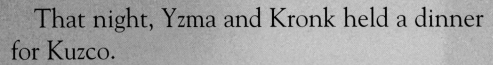

That night, Yzma and Kronk held a dinner for Kuzco.

But, as usual, Kronk goofed. He couldn't remember which cup contained the poison.

At last Kuzco drank.

Then something very strange happened. The emperor grew long ears . . . and fur . . . and hooves! He was turning into a llama!

Yzma told Kronk to knock Kuzco out and get rid of him, once and for all.

Kronk had two little advisers. One was an angel and one was a devil.

"You're not just gonna throw him away, are you?" asked the angel.

"Don't listen to that guy!" said the devil.

Kronk was confused. But he still stuffed Kuzco in a sack and headed for the canal.

Then, after dropping the sack containing Kuzco into the canal, Kronk felt terrible. At the last second, he leaped after the sack, and tried to rescue the llama—er—emperor.

But then Kronk tripped. The sack flew out of his hands and onto Pacha's cart! Before Kronk could catch up, Pacha disappeared into the crowd.

Pacha had no idea that the emperor was in a sack on his cart. He was just glad to arrive home to his wife and two children. But he didn't have the heart to tell them the emperor planned to destroy their village.

When Pacha opened the strange sack on his cart, a funny-looking llama spoke to him.

"Demon llama!" cried Pacha.

"Oh, wait. I know you!" said Kuzco. "You're that whiny peasant!"

Pacha gasped. "Emperor Kuzco?" he asked in disbelief.

22

Jungle Bungle

Boy, was Kuzco surprised to find out he was a llama! He demanded that Pacha take him to Yzma. Kuzco thought Yzma would make him human again.

"Not unless you build Kuzcotopia somewhere else," Pacha replied. Kuzco angrily stomped off into the jungle.

"The jungle is dangerous!" warned Pacha.

"La-la-la!" sang Kuzco, ignoring Pacha. "Not listening!"

After tromping through the jungle for a while, Kuzco came upon a cute little squirrel named Bucky. Bucky kindly offered the emperor an acorn. But Kuzco wasn't very grateful.

"Hit the road, Bucky!" he shouted.

Just then, Kuzco tumbled down a hill, waking a pack of jaguars!

The jaguars chased him to the edge of a cliff.

Just when it seemed like the end for Kuzco, Pacha swung through the jungle on a vine and rescued him. But then they both fell into a river thousands of feet below!

"You call this a rescue?" Kuzco asked.

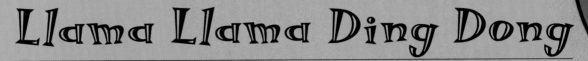

Llama Llama Ding Dong

Meanwhile, back at the palace, Yzma was the new ruler.

"Kuzco is dead, right?" she asked.

"Well—he's not as dead as we would have hoped," Kronk replied.

"You bumbling fool!" shrieked Yzma. Yzma ordered Kronk to take her on a search for the missing emperor–llama.

Night fell in the jungle. Pacha draped his poncho over Kuzco as he went to sleep.

The next morning, Kuzco said something he had never said before in his life: "Uh, thanks."

He also agreed not to destroy Pacha's village to build Kuzcotopia.

Pacha was thrilled!

Of course, Kuzco was lying. He didn't think he needed Pacha anymore. He laughed as Pacha fell through a broken bridge!

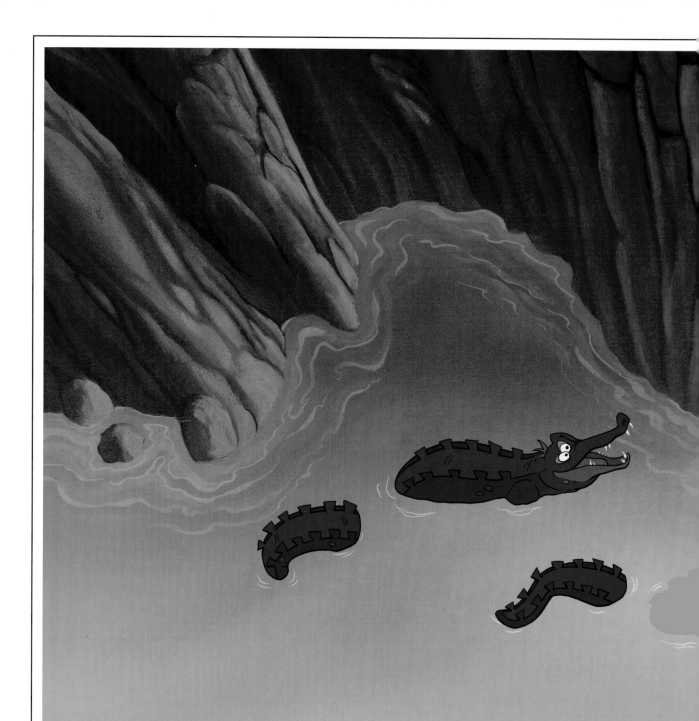

But then Kuzco fell, too! Now they both had to climb back up.

Pacha realized that they would have to work together. Carefully, the two made their way up the cliff.

At the top of the cliff, a piece of rock crumbled under Pacha's feet! Luckily, Kuzco reached out and saved him.

"I knew there was some good in you!" Pacha said.

Meanwhile, Yzma and Kronk met Bucky the squirrel, who told them all about a talking llama.

They knew the llama must be Kuzco.

Kuzco's Shocking Discovery

Pacha took Kuzco, disguised as his bride, to a funky jungle restaurant called Mudka's Meat Hut. "Heeheehee," giggled Pacha as he gave the waitress their order. "We're on our honeymoon!"

Pacha overheard Yzma and Kronk in the restaurant plotting against Kuzco.

"They're trying to kill you!" Pacha warned Kuzco. Kuzco didn't believe Pacha until he overheard them himself.

"If you hadn't mixed up those potions," Yzma said to Kronk, "Kuzco would be dead!" Kuzco was stunned. They *had* tried to kill him.

Alone and frightened, Kuzco ran to find Pacha. But Pacha was gone. For the first time, Kuzco realized how important it was to have a friend.

Later, in the jungle, Kronk awoke from a deep sleep. He remembered that the man in the restaurant—Pacha—was the same peasant he had seen leaving the city with Kuzco on his cart. If they found Pacha, they would find Kuzco!

Kronk, for once, was right: Kuzco *was* with Pacha. Kuzco had found his one true friend among a herd of llamas.

But Kuzco wasn't out of trouble yet! Yzma and Kronk were headed right toward Pacha's house to find Pacha and Kuzco. Luckily, Pacha got his family to stall the evil pair while Pacha and Kuzco headed off to the palace!

Race to the Palace!

It didn't take Yzma long to figure out she had been tricked. She and Kronk caught up with Pacha and Kuzco and chased them through the jungle. When they came to a cliff, Pacha and Kuzco swung to the other side. Kronk and Yzma tried to follow them across, but they were hit by a bolt of lightning. Yikes!

When they finally got to the palace, Kuzco and Pacha raced to the lab. But while they were searching for the potion that would change Kuzco back into a human, Yzma suddenly appeared. "Finish them off!" she told Kronk.

Once again, Kronk was confused. It didn't seem right to get rid of Pacha and Kuzco. So Yzma dropped him through a trap door.

Pacha grabbed the human potion from Yzma.
But the bottle fell to the floor. As Pacha and
Kuzco scrambled to get it, Yzma tipped over
a whole shelf of potions. All the potions
looked the same!

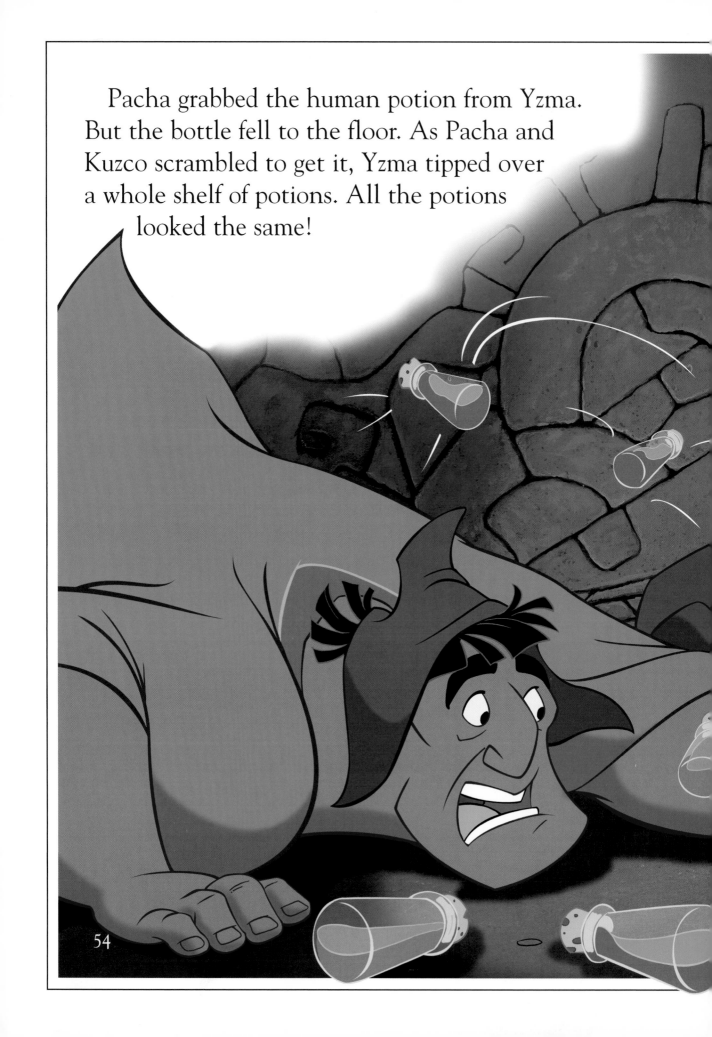

Kuzco to the Rescue

Yzma called the guards, who chased Kuzco and Pacha outside the palace. Kuzco and Pacha had just two bottles left! One would make Kuzco human again. But Yzma got ahold of one of the bottles. It turned her into a cat!

Now they were down to the last bottle! Kuzco knew it must be the one that would make him human again.

Suddenly Pacha slipped. He grabbed onto the palace wall, but was losing his grip. Kuzco had to choose: either take the potion, or save Pacha's life.

Finally, Kuzco actually did the right thing: he saved Pacha. But Yzma had the human potion!

Just then Kronk opened the door, and accidentally flattened Yzma the kitty!

She dropped the potion, and Pacha caught it. Kuzco could finally become human again.

Later, Kuzco decided to build his summer home on a different hill.

Pacha smiled. He knew that Kuzco was sparing his village but was too embarrassed to admit he was doing something nice.

Kronk turned out to be a great camp counselor for all the kids in Pacha's village. With Bucky's help, he even taught them how to speak squirrel.